Sunny Days

by **Trudi Strain Trueit**

Reading Consultant: Nanci R. Vargus, Ed.D.

Marshall Cavendish
Benchmark
New York

Picture Words

 apples

 bikes

 bubbles

 butterflies

 flowers

 ice cream cones

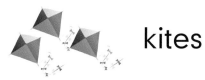 kites

 sun

 trees

The ☀ is out!
We can play!

We can ride
on a sunny day.

We can eat
on a sunny day.

We can pick 🍎🍎🍎
on a sunny day.

We can chase
on a sunny day.

We can pick
on a sunny day.

We can blow
on a sunny day.

We can fly on a sunny day.

We can climb

on a sunny day.

Words to Know

blow (bloh)
   to push air out of the mouth

climb (klime)
   to use your arms and legs to go up

Find Out More

Books

Landau, Elaine. *The Sun*. New York: Scholastic, 2008.

Olien, Rebecca. *Exploring the Sun*. New York: PowerKids Press, 2007.

Winrich, Ralph. *First Facts: The Sun*. Mankato, MN: Capstone Press, 2005.

DVDs

Dimming the Sun. WGBH Boston Video, 2007.

The Sun. Disney Educational Productions, 2004.

Web Sites

Environmental Protection Agency (EPA): SunWise Kids
www.epa.gov/sunwise/kids.html

National Aeronautics and Space Administration (NASA): Sun for Kids
www.nasa.gov/vision/universe/solarsystem/sun_for_kids_main.html

About the Author

Trudi Strain Trueit has always loved weather. A former television weather forecaster for KAPP TV in Yakima, Washington, and KREM TV in Spokane, Washington, Trudi wrote her first book for children on clouds. Since then, she has written more than forty nonfiction titles for kids covering such topics as snow, hail, tornadoes, and storm chasing. Trudi writes fiction, too, and is the author of the popular *Julep O'Toole* series for middle-grade readers. Born and raised in the Pacific Northwest, Trudi lives near Seattle, Washington, with her husband. You can read more about Trudi and her books at **www.truditrueit.com**.

About the Reading Consultant

Nanci R. Vargus, Ed.D., used to teach first grade. Now she works at the University of Indianapolis. Nanci helps young people become teachers. She likes spending sunny days in New York's Central Park with her grandson Oliver.

Marshall Cavendish Benchmark
99 White Plains Road
Tarrytown, NY 10591-5502
www.marshallcavendish.us

J 551.5271 Trueit

Library of Congress Cataloging-in-Publication Data
Trueit, Trudi Strain.
Sunny days / by Trudie Strain Trueit.
        p. cm. — (Benchmark rebus. Weather watch)
Includes bibliographical references.
Summary: "Easy to read text with rebuses explores fun time activities on a sunny day"—Provided by publisher.
ISBN 978-0-7614-4017-8
1. Sun—Juvenile literature. I. Title.
QB521.5.T78 2009
551.5'271—dc22
        2008037271

Editor: Christine Florie
Publisher: Michelle Bisson
Art Director: Anahid Hamparian
Series Designer: Virginia Pope

Photo research by Connie Gardner

Rebus images provided courtesy of *Dorling Kindersley*.

Cover photo by Comstock/Alamy

The photographs in this book are used by permission and through the courtesy of:
SuperStock: p. 5 Mauridus; *PhotoEdit:* p. 7 Michael Freeman; *Jupiter:* p. 9; *Corbis:* p. 11 Hein van de Heuve/zefa;
p. 19 Arid Skelley; *Getty Images:* p. 13 Nancy Falcon; p. 15; p. 21 Stuart Redler; *The Image works:* p. 17 Bill Bachmann.

Printed in Malaysia
1 3 5 6 4 2